Don't interrupt!

kathy Henderson

Illustrations by Sue Hellard

BARRON'S

Jim was thirsty,
Jim was small.
Jim couldn't reach
The faucets at all.

So he asked his mom.

"Mom! Oh please Mom,
Can I have a drink?"
"Don't interrupt. Of course you can.
Now shush and let me think."

So he picked up the stool
And carried it in.
"All right, I'll get it myself,"
Said Jim.

Jim was trying.
Jim had to stretch and hop
But he still couldn't make it
Up to the top.

So he asked his dad.

"I need a drink Dad,
And it's too high up."
But his dad was busy talking.
"Don't interrupt!"

So Jim took the pillow
That was next to the phone.
"Well," he sighed, "I suppose
I can do it alone."

Jim was struggling.
Jim had gone pink
From slipping and sliding
Off the side of the sink.

So he thought he'd try his brother.

"Would you help me Charlie,
'Cause I'm not big enough."
"Not now, I can't miss this !
It's really good stuff !"

So Jim carried off
The cookie box instead.
"I'll just have to do it
By myself," he said.

He stomped back to the kitchen.
"Well there's nothing down here.
I'll just have to climb up
Higher.... Oh dear!"

Jim was tired.
Jim was fed up.
Now the faucet was on,
But there wasn't a cup.

So he went up to his sister.

"You've got all the cups, Annie.
Couldn't I have one?"
"Don't interrupt," said Annie,
"You're spoiling our fun."

Jim had problems.
Jim had started well,
But the goldfish bowl had fallen.
Who could he tell?

So he went to ask the neighbors.

"I'm trying to get a cup
But there's a fish in my shoe."
"Well aren't *you* lucky, dear.
That's very nice for you."

When he went back to the kitchen,
There was no time to lose.
The cat was going fishing
In Jim's soggy shoes.

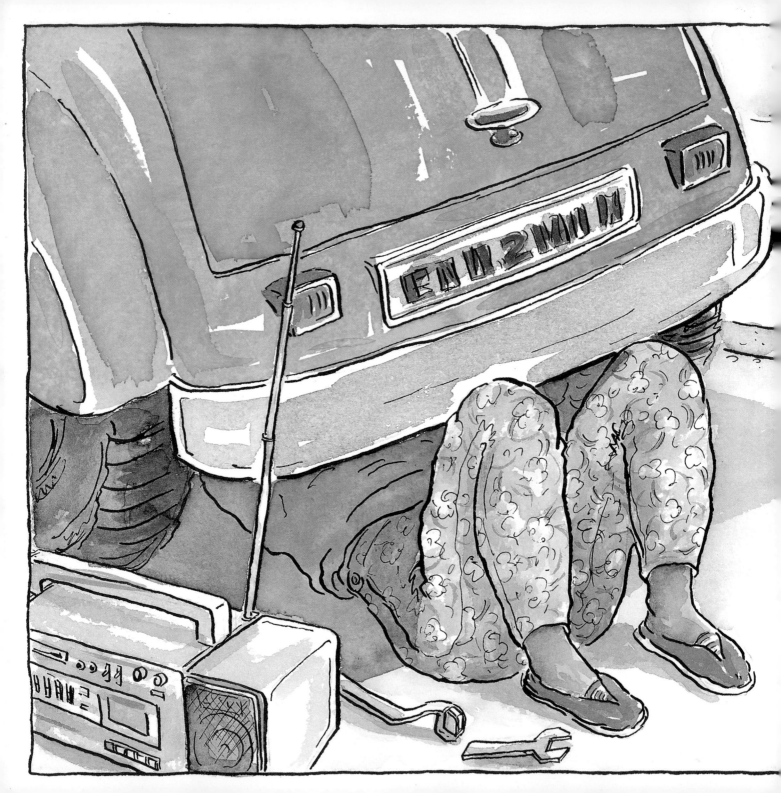

Jim was winning.
The fish was safe and sound,
But the water was splashing
Down onto the ground.

So he went to find Lyn.

"I need a drink, Lyn,
But it's getting very wet...."
"What was that you said?
I can't hear you, pet."

Well they all heard the crash
And came running in.
There were Mom and Dad and Annie
And Charlie and Lyn.

They looked round the door.

"Oh no!" said Mom,
And Dad gave a groan.

"Don't interrupt!" said Jim.
"I did it on my own."